Ca   **Wallace**

That Furball Puppy and Me

Illustrated by Jason Wolff

New York   London   Toronto   Sydney   Singapore

First Aladdin Paperbacks edition February 2002

ALADDIN PAPERBACKS
An imprint of Simon & Schuster
Children's Publishing Division
1230 Avenue of the Americas
New York, NY 10020

Printed in the U.S.A.
4 6 8 10 9 7 5

ISBN: 0-7434-1029-7

To
Kacey and Justin, Nikki and Jon-Ed,
Laurie and Kevin, Bethany and Kristine

That Furball Puppy and Me

CHAPTER 1

Ring . . . Ring."

The loud, shrill noise made my ears twitch.

"Ring . . . Ring."

The sound came from the ringy-box on the wall. It was a strange, little white box that hung in the kitchen. Every time it said, *"Ring . . . Ring,"* the Mama would pick it up and start talking to herself.

Sure enough . . .

Mama left the dishes she was working on in the sink and wiped her hands on the towel. She picked up the little ringy-box and held it against the side of her head.

"Hello," she said to herself. Suddenly a smile crept across her face. "Well, hi." Her tone was light and happy. "It's good to hear your voice, too." Her eyes got big. "Really? You're going to have that much time off at Christmas? How wonderful! Hang on a second." Cupping a hand to the side of her mouth, she turned toward the living room. "Owen, get the other phone. It's the kids!"

The smile on Mama's face stretched from one ear to the other. She grinned and giggled. She leaned against the wall. She turned in circles and got the cord on the ringy-box all wrapped around herself, but Mama never seemed to notice. She just kept talking to herself with the ringy-box against her ear. The more she talked to herself, the more happy and excited she seemed to get.

People were really hard to understand.

I mean . . . well . . . I guess I talked to myself sometimes, too. I didn't get all excited about it. I didn't meow and talk out loud, and I didn't go flittering all over the house. Mostly, I just told myself that I *wasn't* really afraid of the big rats that lived in the barn. I told myself that I was getting stronger and braver each day. Soon I wouldn't be scared of them. They would be scared of me!

That's what Callie told me to do. Callie was the old cat who was already here when I came to live with my new family. She was wise and brave. She knew a whole lot more than I did. Callie told me to keep telling myself how brave and strong I was, and that sooner or later I would believe it. I did. Only I still didn't believe—not really.

Callie also told me that my friend Flea would come back before I knew it. Each day I climbed onto the windowsill in the playroom. The Mama had a feeder that hung from a limb on the pecan tree. I watched out the window as the birds fluttered around. They flittered and hopped from one limb to the next. They chirped and ate the seeds. Sometimes they even flew about and chased each other. But Flea wasn't with them. I kept telling myself that she would come back. When I didn't see her, it made me feel sad inside.

All right . . . I know it's kind of weird for a cat to have a mockingbird as a friend. Flea was different, though. She wasn't just any old mockingbird—she was kind of like my adopted family. When we first met, Flea wanted me to eat her. That was because she was afraid to fly. Her family went "south" without her. She was scared and lonely and so hungry she was about to starve.

Since I don't eat birds, she finally talked me into feeding her instead. I had fun helping her learn to fly. It wasn't easy, but with some help from Callie and Mr. Bullsnake, we finally taught her. She started her trip south a few weeks after the rest of her family. I worried that she might be cold or even lost some place. But Callie promised that she would be fine. She said that Flea would be back. Winter followed fall, and spring followed winter. It was winter. Flea had only been gone a few months, but it seemed to me that winter was forever and spring would never come.

So, I kept telling myself that Flea would be back, and I kept telling myself that I *wasn't* afraid of the big rats.

Only I didn't smile and laugh and get all excited when I talked to myself. Mama was weird.

My tail flipped as I watched her almost dance around the kitchen, holding the ringy-box and jabbering away. The Mama talked to herself for a long time. When she finally put the box back on the wall, she let out a squeal. The Daddy came in and grabbed her in his arms.

"I can't believe it. They'll all be home for Christmas! I can't wait!"

Daddy spun Mama around once, then put her down. He gave her a kiss on the cheek and patted her bottom. Mama pushed his hand away.

"Quit . . . we don't have time for any of your nonsense. There's lots to do and not much time to get ready!" Mama jumped around and started working again.

I looked up at the Mama and Daddy. There was excitement in the house. There was a happy feeling. I liked this. I liked the good feeling.

For a while it seemed as if there was nothing but sad in the house. I was sad because my Flea flew south for the winter. The Mama and Daddy were sad because of Muffy. Muffy was the brown dog who lived in the backyard. She was very old and not very friendly to me. I think it was because Muffy's bones and legs hurt so bad. I think it was because she didn't feel well.

The Mama and Daddy had to take Muffy to the vet. Even before they left the house, the sadness had crept in. They moved slow—as if they really didn't want to go. When they came home, the sad feel in the house was even worse. Water leaked from the Mama's eyes when they came inside. I don't know what happened to Muffy. I don't know why she didn't come home from the vet. I do know that the Mama and Daddy were very, very sad.

Now, for the first time in a long while, they were happy. It made me happy, too. It made me feel good.

Fact was, it made me feel so good that I marched straight to the front door. I put my paws on the wood and meowed as loud as I could.

"Let me out!" I demanded. "Out. Now!"

It wasn't long before Mama came. She leaned down and stroked my head, then she opened the door for me. Feeling bigger and braver and stronger than I had ever felt before, I pranced down the sidewalk. I marched straight to the big barn and stood at the crack between the two giant doors.

The smell of rodents was everywhere. I pushed my head in through the crack. I knew the rats were there. This time I was sure I could handle them.

With a little wiggle, I slipped inside. I paused a moment, letting my eyes get used to the dark. Four large, dark forms sat by the grain bin. Crunching sounds came to my ears. I guess the rats were gnawing on some kernels of corn. A knot kind of stuck in my throat when I swallowed. These creatures were even bigger than I remembered.

I eased closer. The rats didn't seem to notice as I inched toward them. Suddenly two of them spotted me and darted for a hole in the corner.

When they ran, it made me feel big and brave. But . . .

The two other rats stopped eating and looked up. They *didn't* run.

"Hey, Nora. Look at the little kitty cat!"

"Yeah, Smitty. I've seen him before. He's the fraidy-cat, remember?"

The one called Smitty took a step toward me. "Yeah, he's the one we chased. Nearly got him, too. Reckon he's slower now? He's a lot fatter, almost big enough to eat." Smitty licked his lips.

Nora's yellow eyes pierced like hot embers as the two rats glared at me.

My stomach did a flip-flop. I backed slowly toward the door. Both rats inched forward. They moved apart—one came at me from the right, the other from the left. I felt my tail fuzz. It sprang straight up behind me, almost as big around as the rest of me was.

They stopped and stared. Not even their whiskers twitched. Then they moved again, quicker this time. I felt a shiver as I suddenly realized they were trying to surround me. They were trying to block my escape from the big, dark barn.

Without taking my eyes from them, I backed up.

"Now!" Nora hissed in her ratty voice. "Let's get him!"

Chapter 2

Okay . . . maybe I overdid it with the happy feeling. Maybe I needed to talk to myself like Mama
did. Maybe I needed to get more excited and more
worked up. Maybe I needed to spend a little more
time trying to convince myself that I really was
big and brave and strong, before I tried to face
the rats.

I was just lucky I made it through the crack
between the two wooden doors. As big as I was
fuzzed up, I was surprised I managed to make it.
Once safely outside the barn, I headed for the
house and meowed for Mama to let me in.

I checked the cat bowl on the kitchen floor.
Callie had left me a few bits of egg and bacon. I
gobbled them down. People were confusing. The
ringy-box was confusing. And what was this

Christmas stuff? Maybe there were a few more things I needed to figure out before I got too wrapped up in this happy feeling.

The happy in our home seemed to grow with each passing day. Mama left the house more often. She would go to the driveway and start her car. It roared and sputtered. Sometimes when it wouldn't start, Mama would get out and talk mean to it. Then she would try again. One day she even got out and kicked it.

I don't think the car felt it, though. Mama did. She grabbed her foot and started hopping around on her other leg. Then she talked real mean to it again.

Each time Mama left she would come back with lots of packages. The closet was filled with boxes and paper and ribbon. When I was bored, I would investigate the weird things that were hidden away.

One day Mama started bringing all the stuff out. She wrapped colored papers around the boxes. Then she tied on long strings and bows. I watched patiently. When she wasn't looking, I grabbed the ends of the strings that dangled from the side of the packages. I pulled at the bows. I sharpened my long claws on the paper.

"Gray! Bad cat! Get away from the gifts. I'll put you outside!"

I batted at the strings one more time.

Mama picked up one of the long tube things with shiny paper wrapped around it. She whomped me right on the bottom. I scampered away and hid under the couch. Only the ribbons wiggled when the heater came on. The temptation was just too much. When I sneaked back and swatted the string again, Mama picked me up, gave me a quick rub (only she stroked my hair the wrong way), and put me outside.

"You can come in later, Gray."

Cold wind ruffled my hair as I looked around the porch. Callie was still inside. I jumped on the rocker and fluffed my fur, trying to keep warm. There was no sunshine on the porch. It was hard to take a catnap when there was no warm sun to stretch out in. *Boy, is it nippy out here*, I thought.

Leaving the rocker, I jumped to the porch chair and looked in the window. I meowed as loudly as I could. When no one came, I went to the door and scratched at the screen with my claws. Still nobody. My fur kind of gave a little ripple—all on its own. I curled my tail around my legs and sat, watching for someone to open the door.

The sound of a car made my ears twitch. I bounced to the sidewalk to see who it was. The Daddy was getting out of his pickup truck. I hurried to rub against his leg.

"Get back, Gray! I've got to get this tree into the house." He gently shoved me with his foot.

I stood at the end of the driveway and watched. Daddy opened the back of the truck and branches flopped out. I arched an eyebrow. *Guess Daddy ran over a tree. How else would it have fallen into the back of his truck?* He began grabbing the limbs and fighting with the thing. But instead of throwing it away, like I thought he would, he started dragging it toward me.

I scampered up the sidewalk in front of him to keep from getting smushed by the pine tree. Being a cat and getting chased by rats was bad enough. Now a tree was chasing me. I'd never been chased by a tree before.

My fur fuzzed. Eyes wide, I shot for the safety of the pecan tree. This whole thing was getting weirder and weirder. The packages were weird. The ringy-box and the happy feel in the house were weird. The packages, the shiny paper, the string . . . Daddy disappeared through the door. The tree chased right after him. A tree in the house . . . My people were carrying this stuff too far. They were going totally bonkers!

Cautiously, I crept down from the tree and went to the door. I just had to see what was going on. I didn't even have time to put my paws on the screen and peek in when the door flew open. I darted out of the way. Daddy walked toward the barn. I hid under the rocker for a moment, until I felt it was safe, then I went back for a peek. Here came Daddy again. He carried some boards. I scampered for the rocker. Daddy held the door open and bent down to look at me.

"Come on, cat. It's cold out here. Come on in."

I didn't know if I wanted inside or not. I mean . . . what if the tree started chasing me again. What if . . .

"Come on, Gray."

I had to see what was happening. I darted into the house. If I could just make it to my hiding place . . .

Right in the middle of the living room, I came to a screeching stop!

My hiding place was gone! The furniture wasn't where it was supposed to be. A big empty space was in front of the window where the chair belonged. The couch was moved close to the wall. There wasn't any room to squeeze behind it and hide. So I pushed as close to it as I could and watched.

"What's with that stupid cat, Kay? He's been flying around, all puffed up, since I got home. Think he's sick or something?"

"I don't know," Mama called from the kitchen. "Maybe he's just getting into the Christmas spirit. You get the tree?"

"Yeah. Got it inside, already. Where do you want me to put it?"

Mama trotted into the living room. There was a big smile on her face. My whiskers twitched as I pushed myself closer to the wall. I perked my ears, listening to the excited voices.

This was wonderful! Maybe this tree wasn't so bad (now that it was being still and not chasing me). Maybe they brought it inside—just for Callie and me. Sure. That was it. They brought a tree inside for us to climb! I couldn't wait for them to leave so I could scamper to the very top and see what was going on.

Daddy got some boards. He worked with nails and a hammer, trying to get the tree to stand up straight. As soon as it was up, Mama began putting long strings of colorful things around it. She placed them on the tree, frowned, then took them down and started again.

Quietly, I stood up and leaned out from beside the couch. Callie would know what was going on. I crept into the bedroom. She was asleep on a pillow on the bed. Callie didn't even budge when I jumped up beside her. When I meowed, she only twitched her whiskers. I would have to wait. Callie could be cranky when someone woke her up from a sound sleep.

The closet door was open. Inside I could see the packages that the Mama had been wrapping. I hopped down for a closer look. Curiously I sniffed around. Ribbons dangling over the side wiggled when my whiskers brushed against them. I swatted a couple with my paw. The movement was like mice tails scampering away. I grabbed at them. Some of the paper on the outside of the boxes tore. It made me jump back, but for only a second. Then I was right at it again. I couldn't stop! Swat! Rip! I was making a mess, but I just couldn't help myself.

"Gray! What are you doing? I put you outside to keep you from tearing my packages. Here you are, shredding the Christmas presents!"

Mama grabbed me straight up off the floor. Not too sweetly, she carried me to the playroom.

"Sorry, Gray. I can't have you messing up everything. You'll have to stay in here if you can't be a good kitty." She plopped me on the floor and slammed the door behind me.

My tail flipped a couple of times, all by itself, then I sat by the door and listened. The Mama and Daddy talked, their voices excited and happy. There were crinkling sounds and jingling sounds and laughter. I just had to see what was going on in the living room. I lay down on my side. There was a crack under the door. I could see light coming through. I flattened my cheek against the floor so hard that my whiskers felt smushed. If I got my eyeball close enough to the floor, I could see through the crack under the door. Shoving my paw through the opening, I reached and tugged to see if it would open.

Everybody was ignoring me! I meowed as sadly as I could! Still, nobody came.

Finally I hopped up on the couch and curled against the pillow. I kept my ears alert, just in case the door opened. If it ever did, I could be on my feet in a flash. Before the Mama and Daddy could even blink, I would scamper out and see what was happening.

I guess I was sleeping harder than I thought. It startled me when Mama came into the playroom and picked me up. Holding me close, she carried me to the living room.

The tree didn't look like an outside tree anymore. There were tiny lights and shiny things all over it. Long glistening tails circled the branches. My eyes were wide as I tried to see everything. It was beautiful. I just wanted to get down and grab at the stuff hanging from the limbs. Squirming, I tried to get away from Mama.

Below the tree were the packages that I had been playing with. There were lots of new boxes that I had never seen before. I wiggled, trying to get closer for a better look.

Mama squeezed me tighter. "Gray! You're not

getting down. I can't trust you with the decorations and the Christmas presents."

I knew that I was going to get into trouble, but I just couldn't stop!

"Okay, Gray!"

The next thing I knew I was back in the playroom. "Callie," I meowed. "Callie, I need to talk to you. I need you to tell me what's going on. I need to know what all the shiny stuff is and why the tree sparkles and why there's a big bright thing on the top. Callie?"

Callie didn't answer. There was no smell of her near the playroom or in the kitchen on the other side of the door. So I guess she was still asleep on the bed.

The playroom was better than being outside in the cold, but with all the exciting things going on, being trapped in here was the pits.

CHAPTER 3

Let me out of here!" I meowed as loud as I could. Shoving a paw under the door, my sharp claws sank into the wood. I jerked and tugged. The thing rattled, but it wouldn't open.

Something grabbed my paw! It made me yank my leg back. I twisted my head to peek through the narrow opening beneath the door. Callie's fur and one eye were all that I could see.

"Gray, you'd better stop that door rattling. The Daddy will throw you out in the cold. Those sharp claws leave scratch marks in the wood, and the Daddy doesn't like it!"

I stretched my front paw and shook the door again. Callie scampered away.

Whaap! Something hit me on the paw.

I pulled my foot back and peeked under the door.

Daddy's feet were close. A newspaper snapped at the empty space where my paw had been.

"Stop it, Gray!" Daddy yelled at me. "You can come out later. Settle down!"

I crouched near the door so that I could see what was happening. Feet were all that was there. They made a plopping sound when they walked on the hard, shiny floor that went from the back door to the kitchen. I couldn't see the kitchen from where I was, but across the bright floor was the table where Mama and Daddy ate. Beyond that was the living room. The floor, in both places, was covered with the same fuzzy carpet that was in the playroom.

Mama's feet and Daddy's feet seemed to scamper all over the living room and around the table. When they disappeared into the kitchen, I could hear their feet on the floor. I've never felt so much excitement in our home. Suddenly Callie's whiskers and eye appeared again.

"I warned you to quit shaking the door!" Callie flattened her body against the floor.

"What's going on out there? I need to see what's happening."

"It's the day before Christmas, and there is going to be a party in the house. The children and the Grandkids are coming home."

"What are children? What are Grandkids?"

"Children are little Human babies. Only these

babies are grown-ups now and they have some children of their own.''

My head cocked to one side. ''What are Grandkids?'' I frowned.

From the other side of the door, there was nothing but a long silence.

''Callie? What are Grandkids?''

''You'll have to wait and see for yourself.''

''What about the tree in the living room? It looked like a good climbing tree, but Mama put all that stuff on it. And those pretty boxes in the closet . . . What are they?''

The doorbell rang and Callie scampered away without answering. I tried to peer through the space under the door. Callie was gone. The feet were gone, too.

I sat up and wrapped my tail around my feet. Listening, I leaned my sharp ears close to the door. Sounds filled the air. Voices and squeals of happiness were everywhere. I wanted to grab at the door again, but I could wait. It was awfully cold outside, and the Daddy might put me there instead of just yelling at me. So, with nothing else to do, I washed my paws.

All at once the door flew open. I jumped back to keep from getting clunked in the head.

''There he is!'' Small hands grabbed me, swooped me up off the floor, and held me tight. Four new faces stared at me. "Hey, he's cute. Let me hold him."

"No, I've got him!"

"Give him to me!" the voices yelled.

"Go get Callie! She's here somewhere!"

"I want the kitty!" a small girl said.

One of the hands that held me let go and pushed at the little girl's face.

"Mommm . . . eee!" the little girl squealed.

Suddenly Daddy was standing at the door.

"Joshua, put Gray down. He isn't used to kids grabbing at him. He usually stays outside."

"But, Grandpa, he likes me!"

"Put him down. Let him get used to you first. There are lots of things going on here that Gray hasn't ever seen before. He needs a chance to get used to you."

When I touched the floor, my feet couldn't move fast enough to get me out of there. Trouble was, the floor between the playroom and the living room was different from that in the rest of the house. My feet were on the slick, shiny stuff instead of the thick, warm carpet. I ran. Only, my feet just churned. No matter how hard I ran, I didn't go anyplace. All I did was spin. Finally my paws caught!

When I raced through the living room, there were big people everywhere. Packages and stuff were all over the room. What was going on? I had to hide.

I tore down the hall, skidded around the corner, raced past the bathroom door, and into the safety of the bedroom. Gasping for breath, I slid under the bed. The only sound was a loud thumping inside my chest. I flattened myself on the floor and waited. I could hear the sounds of excitement coming from the living room.

"Did they scare you?" Callie's soft purr came from on top of the bed. I stuck my head out and looked up. Callie leaned over the edge.

"They were screaming at me! They were grabbing me. Who are they? What's going on?"

"Those are the Grandkids!" Callie answered. "I don't know how they got that name—*Grand*kids. I never thought they were all that grand. They don't bother me too much anymore. Mama and Daddy make them leave me alone. I think that you are in for some trouble though. Grandkids love little kitties. You're not that little anymore, but to them you're still a kitty."

A tense and nervous feeling shuddered through me. I wanted to run. Where could I go? I ducked back under the bed. My ears were perked, listening to all the racket from the living room. I could hear Callie purring from the pillow on the bed above me.

It wasn't long before Mama came in and

walked over to her. She petted Callie gently. "Gray, where are you, kitty? The kids want to see you. Here, kitty!"

Mama looked under the bed. I backed up quietly. She didn't see me. Holding my breath, I didn't even move.

She petted Callie another time and walked out, still calling my name. I guess I was safe for now.

Smells in the house floated into the bedroom. Except for a tiny bit of leftover eggs and bacon, I hadn't had any breakfast. My tummy growled. How could I get to my food bowl with those short, grabby little people in there? I had to have something to eat. The smells coming from the kitchen were wonderful. They made my mouth water. I had to get to my food bowl.

I had seen danger before. I had been attacked by a mean rooster when I was a baby. I had looked eye to eye with a *big* rat. I would have to face the . . .

Grandkids!

CHAPTER 4

Bravely I stepped out from under the bed. Taking a deep breath, I held it and listened for any sound of danger. Inch at a time, I crept to the door. The Grandkids were here, somewhere. I stayed close to the wall until I got to the living room. If I was careful, I could hide behind the furniture until I reached the kitchen. That's where my food bowl was. Just thinking about it made my tummy rumble.

At the end of the hall I stopped. The tree was in front of me. The bright lights twinkled like little stars. Shiny balls tempted me to bat at them. The long strings dangled and wiggled like mouse tails scampering away in the hay field.

The people were all at the table. My head tilted to the side and my whiskers twitched. The table was *huge*. It was a lot longer than ever before. Maybe Mama watered it like her houseplants to make it grow. Now that it was big, there was room for everyone's chair. Mama and Daddy were near one end. Four other big kids were sitting with them. The Grandkids sat together at the other end of the table.

I eased behind the couch. The tree caught my attention again. The temptation was too much. I carefully tapped at the gleaming bauble in front of my eyes. It moved. I tapped it again. It bounced and jiggled at the end of the limb. I couldn't stop! Each time I batted at the beautiful things, they moved, just like when I chased mice.

"Hey, there's that kitty!"

Small feet thundered through the living room toward me. Small hands grabbed at me.

Like a shot, I scampered up the tree!

"Oh, my goodness!" Mama screamed.

The tree began to wobble. I moved higher. The tree swayed. My sharp claws dug at the wood, trying to keep my balance.

"Kay, get on the other side, and we'll get him before he knocks the whole thing over!" Daddy grabbed at the center of the tree.

Mama was not very gentle when she yanked me out of the decorated limbs. But once in her arms, she rubbed me tenderly and pulled me close to hear my purr.

"Let's put him in the playroom."

"I don't think he has eaten today, Owen. That may be why he is being so wild. Let me get him some turkey scraps. Then he can go back to the playroom."

Mama tucked me under one arm as she walked to the kitchen. She placed some yummy meat in my dish. Then she poured this warm brown sauce all over it. The food smelled *wonderful!* I wiggled, struggling to get down. Mama squeezed me tighter under her arm. She took me and my bowl into the playroom and closed the door. I didn't even try to follow her. I went straight to the yummy-smelling food. It was so good that I kept eating, even after I was full. When I finished, I washed my face and paws. A warm, happy feeling covered my whole body.

Trouble was, it didn't last long.

The door flew open. Out of nowhere, small hands picked me up. Suddenly I was on my back with my feet sticking straight up in the air. The pudgy little hands rubbed my fat tummy.

"Be careful, Kensey." Mama warned. "Gray isn't used to children. He has sharp claws and you could get a scratch."

The small girl turned me right-side-up and looked me straight in the eye. She rubbed behind my ears and under my chin. *Hey, this isn't so bad,* I thought. Fact was, it felt pretty good. I closed my eyes. Maybe Grandkids weren't so horrible after all.

A noise made my eyes open. They flashed wide when I saw three more faces staring at me.

"Let me have him, Kensey. You're too little to hold the cat. Give him to me!"

"No, I like the kitty. He likes me, too! Look at him. He's happy!"

"Give me the cat! I'm the oldest. I want to hold him!"

Gentle hands suddenly turned rough. I felt tugs on my fur and skin.

"Momm . . . eee . . ."

"Josh, leave Gray alone. If you can't play nicely with him, I'll have to put him outside. Kensey can pet him for a while, then Jenny and Katie will have time to hold him. You're the oldest and you know you have to take turns." Mama handed me back to the little girl. She carried me into the living room and sat down on the couch.

The rest of the people came in there, too. Feeling restless and nervous with all these strangers around, I tried to wiggle away. The little girl held me tighter.

"I wanna be Santa," the boy yelped.

"Josh, sit down and be quiet!" one of the big people said in a deep, growly voice. "You know Grampa always gets to be Santa."

"Can I open my presents first, then?"

"We'll take turns, just like always." A woman spoke in a soft, gentle voice.

"Well, if I can't play Santa and if I can't open my presents . . . I want to hold the kitty."

"No! It's still my turn."

The little girl squeezed me so tight, I thought my eyes were going to pop out.

"Joshua!" The big man with the gruff voice glared at the boy. His look reminded me of the way the Daddy looked at me when I climbed the tree. The boy sat back down and folded his arms. His bottom lip stuck out. For a moment or two everyone was quiet. Slowly, Daddy walked to the tree. He bent down and picked up one of the packages.

"Let's see. The first one is for . . ." All the people seem to straighten and suck in a deep breath. They held it while he peeked inside a little piece of paper on top of the package. "Well, I'll be," he said finally. "It's for Joshua."

The little boy bounced up and down on the couch when Daddy handed him the package. Then Daddy took another and another from under the tree and handed them to the people in the room. The little girl, who was holding me and giving me a nice rub, didn't take her package. So Daddy put it down beside her.

When everyone had a package, Daddy stood in

the middle of the room. He looked all around and took a deep breath.

"Okay," he said. There was almost a laugh in his voice. "Ready. Set. Go!"

I never heard such a commotion in my life!

All of a sudden there was a tearing, ripping sound. Papers and ribbons flew from the presents. The girl released me. There was more ripping and tearing and talking and laughing. Bright paper fluttered to the floor and ribbons flew. It was like a roar. Before I could make it off the couch and run, another set of hands grabbed me.

This girl looked me over carefully. I struggled to get away. I wanted to run. I wanted to hide. She stroked my fur and talked real soft to me. It made me relax a bit, but I still wanted down. Ribbons and paper and string cluttered the floor and the furniture.

"Jenny, it's okay to let Gray down. He can't tear up anything now. We'll just have to make sure that he doesn't climb up in the tree again."

The girl put me on the floor and rubbed my fur the wrong way. It made my tail flip. I pulled away and hid behind the tree.

I didn't hide for very long. There was too much going on—too much excitement. I reached out to bat at the shiny things again. The little people pulled strings in front of me. My claws popped out when I tried to catch them.

Josh, the biggest little kid, rolled paper up into a ball and nudged it in front of me. I slapped at it. It rattled and tumbled away. I batted and scampered after it all the way across the floor. I chased the paper ball until I was exhausted.

Finally I jumped onto the couch with Mama. She held me in her lap. I closed my eyes. I had to keep listening though. The Grandkids would grab at me if I wasn't careful.

I must have dozed off. When my eyes opened, the room was much quieter. The Grandkids were nowhere in sight. Mama rubbed my fur and stroked under my chin.

"Gray, it's almost time for Santa to come. You'll have to spend another night in the playroom!"

Mama set me on the chair in the corner. As soon as she turned out the light and shut the door, I dashed to my litter box. I ate so much yummy meat at dinnertime, I was afraid I was going to bust.

When I was done, I scratched at the litter. Bits of fine gravel flew everywhere. Sometimes Mama would get upset when she found kitty litter all over the floor. I didn't understand. All good kitties cover up their messes. So I got a little carried away. I flicked my ears. It was no big deal. I went back to the door. My sharp ears picked up sounds.

Paper crinkled. There were whispers, then a grinding sound. *Grrr* . . .

Someone giggled.

"Josh is going to love this one," someone else whispered.

I couldn't tell who was talking. I couldn't see anyone there when I looked under the door. I wondered if it was the Santa that everyone was talking about. Who is Santa?

And where were we going to put him? The house was full enough already. There were too many people. There was too much stuff! A cat couldn't walk for all the mess in the house.

CHAPTER 5

Morning sounds came from the kitchen. I peeked under the door. Feet shuffled past my view. The smell of coffee came to my nose.

"It looks like the kids got tons of stuff from Santa," Daddy said.

"Yeah, what a mess!" Girl's feet as big as Mama's moved to the table. "I hope we can find room for all these things in the van!"

"Let me *out!*" I reached my paw under the door. I grabbed the wood and gave it a good shake.

"Heather, will you please let Gray out? I don't think he can make any bigger mess than what we already have here."

The door opened. The girl with the Mama-size feet reached down and swooped me up.

"Hey, Gray, you put up with a lot yesterday. What a good kitty you are!"

I stretched my neck trying to look around the room and see what had happened last night. I rubbed my face against the big girl's cheek. While I was there, I peeked over her shoulder and into the living room.

"Okay, kitty, you can go." The girl set me on the floor.

I walked toward where the big tree stood, tall and beautiful. The papers that I had played with last night were missing. Ribbons and bows were gone, too! Under the tree new boxes covered with colorful wrapping were spread out on the floor.

Stepping carefully, I moved closer to the tree. Three tiny girls in beautiful dresses sat under a branch. A little car and clothes were strewn out on the floor. I walked up cautiously. I looked the little girls directly in the eyes. They stared straight ahead. I rubbed against them. They didn't budge. I sniffed the little car. It didn't budge, either.

Curling up under the tree, I watched the movements above. The lights on the limbs twinkled. I put my chin on my paws and studied all the wiggly things.

"Heather, why didn't you wake me?" A kid as big as Daddy walked to the table. He leaned down and kissed the big girl.

"Since you were up so late last night, I thought you needed the sleep."

"I think the kids are awake. I heard a lot of whispering in the girls' room. Josh was getting dressed, but I told him to stay put until everyone was ready in here."

"I'll get Paul and Dana up, before we let the kids loose." Mama walked to the hall and disappeared toward the bedrooms.

Squeals of happiness suddenly filled the house. Two big kids staggered down the hall. Excited voices shouted toward the living room.

"Everybody's up, now. We're ready to come out! Let us out!" The Grandkids were yelling as loud as they could.

"Who woke them up?" the big boy people growled. "I've got to have some coffee before they come in!"

"You'd better hurry. Josh has been awake for a long time!"

Mama handed Dana and Paul mugs of coffee.

I scooted farther back under the tree. The Grandkids would be after me very soon.

Noises grew louder from the bedroom. Squeals and giggles, then whines of despair. (The sound was weird—more like play whines than really unhappy.) I wasn't sure what would happen next, but I was hidden where they couldn't get their hands on me.

In a few minutes the big boy, called Carl, finally walked to the hallway.

"Okay, Josh, bring Kensey, Jenny, and Katie in! Everybody's ready!"

The rest of the family was standing near the kitchen.

As soon as the Grandkids stepped into the living room flashes of light lit up everything. I turned my head to see where it came from. Mama and Daddy were holding boxes in front of their faces. I was looking right at Mama when her light flashed. It was so bright it made me blink. When I opened my eyes, all I could see was a blue dot. It went away quickly. I decided to watch the Grandkids instead of the light boxes.

The Grandkids stood still for a few minutes, then yells and squeals filled the air. Each one of them ran to a pile of things under the tree. Nobody seemed to notice me.

I was safe in my spot for a long time. The Grandkids ripped open presents and tore boxes. They looked at each gift carefully then set it in a pile beside them. Then they turned to open another box. The house was a mess again.

"Breakfast is ready," Mama called.

The living room was suddenly empty. I ventured from my hiding spot. I carefully worked my way toward the kitchen. Callie had left me plenty of tender cat food in the bowl.

"I think there is one more present that Santa left." Carl got up from the table and headed for the front door. "I am sure there is one more gift out here!"

When Carl came back inside, he was carrying a big box with holes in it. He pushed the empty boxes and paper away from under the tree and set it down as the family came back into the living room.

"Look, Mama. It's for you!"

I stood near the kitchen door. Sounds of scratching came from the box. This was a bad sign.

Mama frowned at the box just like I did. A whining sound came from inside, then more scratching. Mama tilted her head to the side. I felt my tail puff—just a little—but I didn't know why. My ears wiggled when I turned to look at it.

Mama reached for the big red bow. Before she touched it, the box began to wiggle.

"Yap, yap!" the box said.

My tail fuzzed up even bigger as a strange, shrill sound came from the wiggling box.

If I thought the Grandkids were bad, they were nothing compared to this . . . Mama's present.

CHAPTER 6

The Grandkids squealed. The big kids all moved toward the box. It wiggled. Then it bounced. Then it almost tipped over.

"Yap, yap!" the box said.

"Look, Mama! Look what Santa brought you!"

Mama leaned over and peered into the box. Then she turned to Daddy.

"Oh my gosh! A puppy!" Mama smiled. Then she got this sort of helpless look on her face. She smiled again, then frowned. "Is it a puppy or a big rat? What is he?"

Did she say rat? I jumped to the back of the couch.

Mama knelt down and pulled something from the box. The children and Grandkids pressed closer.

"We knew how much you missed Muffy. Santa brought you a new puppy."

"But what is it?"

"It's a Scottish terrier," Carl said.

Mama frowned. "I didn't know they were white. The ones I've seen are black. Are you sure it isn't a big rat?" Mama smiled as she held the squirming, fuzzy beast up for a better look.

"We're sure!" The big kids all spoke at once.

It was the first time I got a good look at it. It was white and fuzzy and as ugly as could be. It had this long pink tongue that kept flopping out of its mouth when it tried to lick Mama's hand. And the back end of the thing kept wiggling so hard, I thought it might shake apart. (At least, I think it was the back end. Mostly the thing was just fuzz and fluff. It was hard to tell the front from the back.)

"Isn't he cute!" Heather sat down next to Mama. Dana moved nearer. I jumped to the top of the big wooden chest near the kitchen door. I needed a better view, out of reach of this big rat!

Curling my tail around me, I licked my paws and washed my face. I kept one eye on the fuzzy, wiggly, little beast below me.

The Grandkids were laughing and petting it, all at the same time. Each one pushed to get closer.

It was hard to see what this animal really

looked like with all the family gathered around it.

"Okay, kids, it's time to give Grandmother a chance to hold her puppy by herself. Go get your stuff and leave them alone for just a little while." Carl scooted the Grandkids toward the bedroom doors. He kind of held his arms out and waved them—like Daddy did when he was herding cows in the big lot behind the barn.

"Go play with your toys. The playroom will be a good place. Give your grandmother just a while."

"Awww gee, Dad! He's so cute." Josh looked up at Carl. "Can I take him outside when Grandma gets through playing with him?"

"Sure, son, but *later!*" He jabbed a sharp finger toward the bedroom. "Now, scat. Take the girls and go play for a while."

"Okay! Come on, Kensey! Jenny and Katie get her hands." The Grandkids bounced toward the hallway.

I didn't like the looks of the thing on Mama's lap. It was horrible! The animal was covered with shaggy white fur. Even its eyes were hidden by the long fuzz. Its short legs shook in the air as Mama gave it a nice tummy rub. It was disgusting. I could use a good rub, but instead, the beast got one.

I jumped down from the chest, then walked over and rubbed against the door.

"Mee . . . ow! I need some fresh air."

"Will somebody let that cat out?" Daddy called from the kitchen.

When the door opened, I slid out as quickly as I could. Cold air shook my whiskers as I stepped to the end of the porch. There was no sunshine. Just another cold and dreary day.

There was this strange white covering all over the ground. I frowned. When I stepped off the porch it went crunch under my paws. I yanked my foot back and looked. I touched it with my tongue. The white stuff was cold but tasted just like rainwater. Whatever the stuff was, it wasn't bad—just cold.

I checked all of my favorite spots. The apple tree. The woodpile. The holly bushes. I even peeked into the barn. Three rats were in a corner eating grain. Nora, the big rat, glared up at me. Okay . . . time to go back in with my people. At the front of the house I jumped to the ledge under the window.

"Meee . . . ow! I need in! It's cold out here. Me . . . ow!" I could see the little furball asleep on Mama's lap. That should be me—all warm and cozy!

I jumped down and scratched on the door. When it opened, I dashed in and ran for the bedroom. Like usual, Callie was asleep on the pillow.

"Hey, Callie! Wake up! There is a new animal in the house. It's on Mama! She likes it. I don't! What are we going to do?"

Callie opened one eye. "Relax, Gray. It's only a puppy. They needed a dog to protect the yard. Muffy used to watch for coyotes, but she's gone now! They'll put it outside later." She sighed and nestled her cheek into the pillow. "Puppies are kind of pesky, but right now, you're safe up here. He's too short to jump up this high! Chill out! Curl up! Take a nap!"

Callie wasn't any help at all. A wiggly, fuzzy, yapping furball puppy was in *my* Mama's lap and Callie wanted me to take a nap!

The day was filled with excitement and happiness. Smiles and laughter were everywhere. Only, I wasn't happy. I didn't know why. There was this strange feeling inside of me every time I looked at the little furball. It made my tail flip. I didn't like it. When they finally put the dog out in the yard, I felt a lot better. That part was wonderful! It was almost like it hadn't come here in the first place.

When it got dark, the excitement seemed to get all mixed up with sadness. The kids and the Grandkids began to pack up their stuff. They said that they had to leave in the morning so that they could get back to work. The living room was piled with boxes and suitcases.

I tried to stay on the back of the couches and chairs when someone let the puppy in the house. The thing made this terrible yapping sound. He waggled his back end and scampered all over the place. It was safer up high. When the house settled down, Mama put towels in a big box and set it on the back porch. Then the puppy was put out for the night . . . they stuck me in the playroom.

Clicking sounds hit against the window. I jumped on the windowsill to look out. The bird-feeder swayed in the breeze. Small pieces of white hit against the window. I watched as it began to cover the ground.

"Yap, yap," the puppy yelled. "Help me! It's cold out here! Let me in!"

The yapping went on for a long time. I heard him begging to come into the house. I hopped down and peeked through the crack.

Mama finally went to the door.

"Hey, pup. It's okay. Just stay in the box. We have lots of towels and blankets in there. Settle down. You're okay."

"Yap, yap. I miss my mother. She was so soft and warm. Let me in."

Mama closed the door gently. As I peeked

through the opening, I could still see her house shoes. Daddy's bare feet moved near.

"Are you going to leave him outside?"

"I don't know. I really don't think we need a house dog. We have Gray. He comes and goes, but old Callie might be a problem. She is used to being left alone. The puppy would be all over her. I don't know what to do."

"Yap, yap! It's really cold out here. I need my warm mother! Let me in!" The yapping sound kept going and going.

The Mama and Daddy opened the door. Mama picked up the ball of fluff.

"He's shaking!" Mama pouted and snuggled the furball close. "Look, it's snowing out there. No wonder he's cold. The towels can't keep the dampness away from him."

Daddy's toe pointed toward where I was watching from under the door.

"How about the playroom? Gray will leave him alone. We can put papers down and bring the box of towels inside for him to snuggle. I read that a ticking clock will comfort puppies. It's supposed to remind them of their mother's heartbeat, or something like that." Daddy's feet moved away, toward the hall.

The door swung open. If that ugly beast was going to be in here—I wasn't. I tried to slide past the foot that Mama put in my face. "Get back, Gray!"

When I couldn't get out, I ran to the couch. I hopped on the back, then onto the window ledge. The ball of fluff ran after me.

"Yap, yap! I want to play." He stood on two back legs. His front legs wiggled and shook *my* couch. "Let me up! I want to play!"

Mama stood for a long time watching. She picked the puppy up in her arms and snuggled him. Then she put him in the box.

He didn't stay.

She caught him and put him in the box once more. He hopped out again. When she put him back the last time, she got a big cushion from the couch and put it on the box as a lid.

"Settle down, pup. The whole house is going to be up if you don't get quiet!"

The door shut. I was trapped. The dog whined and whined. He bounced against the box. It rocked back and forth. The cushion wobbled, then fell off. Wiggling and squirming, the white ball of fluff tumbled out of the box. Then . . .

He came straight for me.

This was the night I moved to a new level in the house. *Up!*

CHAPTER 7

I stayed on the back of the couch most of the night. I didn't get a bit of sleep. Every time I so much as thought about dozing off, the puppy would bounce against the bottom of the furniture. He shook my couch and tried to get his short front paws up to the seat. He scratched against the bottom cushion. He chased his tail and yapped.

"Yap, yap, play with me!" he cried.

I tried to ignore him. Maybe he would go away. At least maybe he would go to sleep.

"Yap, yap, I miss my mother. I miss my brothers and sisters."

I curled up on the back of the couch and watched out of one eye. The puppy didn't give up. Finally he perked his ears and went to the door.

"Yap, yap! Let me out! I want to play."

The puppy jumped up against the door. Clawing at the wood, he continued yapping. Callie had warned me about scratching on the door. But I didn't tell the little white ball of fur. Instead, I decided to watch and see what would happen if the puppy kept it up.

It was just a few minutes before the door flew open. Daddy stood over the small pup. He slapped a newspaper against the palm of his hand.

It didn't scare the puppy—not one little bit. He jumped up against Daddy's leg. Daddy smacked the newspaper again. The white furball just bounced all over the place. Daddy reached down and lifted him up so he could look him square in the eye.

"Listen, dog. We've got to get some rest here. Settle down and go to sleep." He put the beast back into the box and replaced the cushion over the top.

The puppy must have been pretty tired. He soon settled down into the towels at the bottom of the box.

I fell asleep, listening to the clicking of the white stuff against the window.

Before it even got light, sounds began coming from the living room. I crept past the box full of puppy. I peeked under the door. A whole bunch of feet were scurrying around. I reached my paw under and pulled at the wood. Feet shuffled nearer.

Mama opened the door and scooped me up. She shut the door quietly.

"Are you trying to wake up the puppy?" Mama glared me in the eye. The next thing I knew I was out on the front porch.

Quickly I took care of my business and hurried back to wait for someone to let me in.

I hopped up on the window ledge and looked inside. People moved around. They bumped into one another, smiled, talked, then scurried about some more.

Suddenly the door opened. I tried to sneak in. A foot pushed me back outside. I jumped on the rocker and fluffed my fur to keep warm.

Carl and Paul carried boxes and suitcases to the driveway. They made lots of trips back and forth. Just as the sky began to brighten, Dana and Heather bundled the Grandkids up in coats, hats, and gloves. Then they brought things that had been in the boxes under the tree and stuffed armloads of toys and presents into their pudgy little hands. At last the whole group headed down the sidewalk. Mama and Daddy followed them out. I hopped down and walked to the end of the yard, where I could see what was going on.

After hugs and kisses and more talking, the

kids and Grandkids piled into a car or a van. When they drove away, Mama and Daddy walked toward the front door.

"Come on, Gray. Let's go in!" Mama grabbed me up in her arms. I could sense a sad feeling on Mama.

Once inside I got a good tummy rub. Mama even got the brush and stroked my fur until I was silky and shiny. The sad feeling was still there. I could feel it everywhere. I explored the bedrooms where the kids and Grandkids had been. The rooms looked nice and neat, but the emptiness felt strange. I had never noticed it before. The rooms seemed to be too quiet without Josh, Jenny, Katie, and Kensey!

Then the empty and quiet was gone—replaced by this loud, shrill, irritating *yapping* sound. All at once the puppy came flying down the hall, just as I was walking to the living room.

"Get him, Owen!" Mama said. "He needs to go outside this morning before he does something on the floor. I couldn't see any messes in the playroom, so I know that he needs to go out!"

Suddenly the puppy spotted me. His eyes got big around.

"Back off, Bozo!" I bared my teeth and hissed. His tongue hung out the side of his fuzzy face as he charged toward me.

Daddy grabbed the puppy. I stepped back just in time.

As soon as they were outside, I hurried to the food bowl to see what Callie had left me. I gobbled down the tender morsels of cat food. The dog would be back, and I had to hurry to a good spot where he wouldn't see me.

The window ledge behind the couch was my favorite hiding place. The curtain hid me from view. I liked looking out at the bird feeder. Snow covered the top of it. Winter birds clustered around, fussing over each little seed. The yard was covered in white.

"I think we need to get the tree down, before the puppy and Gray are in here for very long." The Mama carried boxes to the couch. She began taking small things from the tree. Each one was wrapped, then set in a box. The long strings of shiny lights were wrapped and put away, too.

When there was nothing but an empty tree, Daddy carried it out the front door.

Mama got the puppy and gave it a good rub. Daddy sat down with them and squeezed a squeaky toy. When he rolled it across the floor, the puppy hopped down. He didn't land very well. His front feet kind of folded in under him, and he smushed his face against the carpet. Talk about a klutz. He didn't stay on his nose for very long. He jumped up and chased the squeaky toy across the floor. Then he chased his tail. I watched from my hiding spot.

For a while the sad feeling left our house. Mama and Daddy smiled as they watched the puppy bounce around the living room. When the furball finally got tired, Mama picked him up again and sat near the fireplace. She snuggled him on her lap.

It was quiet as I watched it snow all day long. The puppy seemed to sleep a lot. Mama and Daddy just sat around most of the time.

"I think we need to let the puppy stay in the kitchen tonight. I'll put up something to keep him from getting out, kind of like the baby fence that we used when the kids were little. That way Gray can get out if he needs to."

Mama got up and headed for the playroom. She searched in the closet looking for something.

She came out carrying some big pieces of cardboard. Propping them up against the cabinet and the wall, she divided the kitchen from the dining room.

At bedtime Mama put the box of towels in the kitchen. She and Daddy, both, spread newspapers all over the floor. A step stool, the box, and a bowl of water were the only things left in the room. The puppy and I were put in last. I went to the stool and jumped to the top step. The puppy lay still in the box for a long time.

I was almost asleep when the whining started. The puppy whimpered quietly, at first. "I really like to have you near," he said with a sigh.

I ignored him.

The box wiggled. A black button nose and two little eyes peeked over the edge of it. "I really miss my mama and my brothers and sisters. They played with me all the time."

Still trying to ignore him, I turned my head and curled up on the kitchen stool. The box rattled. I opened one eye. Two, sharp-pointed white ears stuck up over the edge. They bounced up and down.

"I can get out of here," he yapped. "You want to see? I can get out and we can play. You want to play with me? Huh? Want to?"

Standing up and arching my back, I yawned. My whiskers tilted up on one side as I sneered down at him.

"I don't want to play. Go to sleep."

"Oh, please," he whined. "I'm not sleepy. I'm lonely. Let's play."

I flipped my tail and jumped from the stool to the cabinet. "Leave me alone."

Fuzzy paws banged against the side of the box. "That was cool! I wish I could jump like that. How did you do that?"

Instead of answering, I flopped on the kitchen counter and yawned. Why was this guy being such a pest? Everybody knows cats are great jumpers. Why doesn't he just shut up and go to sleep?

The box rocked again when the puppy bounced against the side. Then it tilted and fell over. The furball rolled out, stood, and shook himself. He looked up at me, then bounced against the cabinet doors. There was a sudden "splash" sound. I lifted my head and peeked over the edge of the counter.

With all the bouncing he was doing, the dumb mutt stuck his foot in the water bowl. It splashed all over the place. The papers were wet. His foot was wet. If he kept this up, the whole kitchen was going to be a mess.

Suddenly the whiskers on both sides of my face sprang up.

The whole kitchen was going to be a mess. The words seemed to echo inside my head. If the puppy made a mess, the Mama and Daddy would be mad. When they got mad at me, they put me outside. If the puppy was outside, Mama would have more time to pet me. She could give me more tummy rubs instead of petting the puppy. I loved my tummy rubs.

Quietly I got to my feet. I turned and sat on the edge of the counter, dangling the tip of my tail over the side. The puppy jumped against the cabinet door. I wiggled my tail again. He bounced and tried to nip at it. Sure enough, when he jumped and barked, his little fat hind paws plopped into the water bowl. Water splashed everywhere. He didn't even seem to notice he was all wet. The dumb thing did it again. His soggy feet tracked all over the place.

This really was fun! I jumped to the floor. The puppy chased me around the room. Papers jumbled and crumpled into piles. When I leaped back on the counter, the furball tried to catch his own tail. It made the mess even worse. I waited until he quit, then hopped to the floor again. Eyes wide, here he came. Just as he got close, I hopped on the cabinet. The puppy leaped and bounced against the drawers.

"I'm tired," he panted finally. "I'm sleepy."

I looked down at the mess on the floor. The kitchen was a disaster. Something inside of me gave a little twinge. I don't know what it was. I wanted Mama to be with me—not to spend all her time with the puppy. But the little mutt was so dumb and so trusting and so . . . well . . . so . . .

Who cares? He's just a dumb mutt anyway.

I hissed and fuzzed up my fur to get his attention. The chase game started all over again. I loved to watch him spin around chasing his own tail.

Just before the sky lightened up, I jumped over the barrier and hopped up to the safety of the

couch. Tucked in a ball, with my tail around my face, I went to sleep. The dumb furball must have finally worn himself out. From the kitchen I could hear him pant for a while, then he went to sleep, too.

I was really snoozing when Mama got up to make her coffee. The little squeal that she let out startled me. My eyes popped wide. Mama's mouth was open, as wide as my eyes, when she stood and looked at her kitchen.

"Good grief! What happened in here?"

Quickly I closed my eyes again and tried to pretend I was still sleeping.

There was a scraping sound when Mama moved the cardboard barrier between the kitchen and the living room. Her feet stomped across the floor. I peeked from one eye, just in time to see her spat the puppy on his fuzzy little rump. Then she put him out back and slammed the door.

"Just look at what that dog did! He must have been up all night. He's going to have to stay outside. I don't have time to clean up a mess like this every day!"

"Yap! Yap! Let me in! It's cold out here. I need in!" Small puppy claws hit against the door.

"You didn't have anything to do with this, did you, Gray?" I stayed as still as I could when Daddy walked toward me.

"Of course not!" Crossing my paws in front of me and yawning, I tried to purr as loud as I could.

Daddy tilted his head to the side and looked at me through squinty eyes. "You need to go out anyway, mister." Daddy picked me up and put me out the front door.

Cold north wind hit me in the face. Shaking, I stood near the end of the porch. I fluffed up my fur, trying to keep warm. I could hear the puppy whining and whimpering in the backyard. My plan worked. He was out of *my* house.

But for some reason I didn't feel as good as I thought I should. I mean, why wasn't I happy?

The yard was still covered with snow. It was cold and stuck to my paws. The sky was gray and gloomy. With a jerk of my tail, I stood up straight and tall. *You did good, Gray*, I told myself. Trying to feel proud and happy (but not quite feeling that way), I marched off to check out my favorite places.

When I got back, Callie was on the rocking chair. She did not look happy.

CHAPTER 8

Callie growled low in her throat. "What did you do to that poor puppy? Mama shut him up in that little pen way out in the backyard. She didn't even talk to him when she left." Callie flattened her ears against her head. "She threw *me* out while she cleaned up the mess!"

I flipped my tail in the air and turned my back on her. "I helped him tear up the kitchen. It was fun! I love watching that stupid mutt run around in circles chasing his tail!"

"You should be ashamed of yourself, Gray! That little dog is just a baby. He hasn't been away from his mother very long. Can't you remember how you felt when *you* first came here? You were pretty lonely trying to figure out how things worked in this house. It wasn't that long ago when *I* had to teach you about the house rules."

Callie tried to fluff her thin fur against the icy wind. She looked away from me into the cold white yard. I wiggled my whiskers.

"It was fun! Besides, that dog is taking *my* time away from Mama. She sits and rubs that stupid ball of fur when I should be getting tummy rubs. I want my time back. It's my house, not that dumb puppy's!"

Callie shook her head. "You'd better think about this. You may be the one outside all the time. You're not a baby anymore. The puppy is. Besides that, the house is big enough for all of us. I've shared with lots of other dogs and cats. It takes a little getting used to, but Mama and Daddy have more than enough rubs to go around!"

The snow crunched when I stepped from the porch. My warm paws made some of it stick to my feet.

"Well, it worked didn't it? The puppy is out!"

Callie's tail flipped from side to side. "I guess it did! But we're out, too!"

Callie's glare followed me as I walked toward the pine trees. I would take a quick mouse hunt. Mama would be happy to find a nice trophy on the porch!

My ears perked as I crept closer to the trees.

The mice were hiding under the pine needles and snow. Crouching as low as I could, I wiggled my body closer to the soft mouse sounds. One little mouse was snuggled near the tree trunk. He stayed hidden under the brush. I slapped at the spot where I thought the mouse was. He must have been fast, as I only scooped up sharp needles into my paw. It hurt. With my teeth I pulled the things out. I backed up and shook the snow from my fur.

For a long time I chased mice in the pine trees. The thick blanket of needles and snow helped protect the few mice that were hidden there. When I grew tired, I headed back toward the porch.

The tip of Callie's tail was all that I saw disappearing into the house. The door shut behind it. Jumping up on the window ledge, I meowed as loudly as I could. The fireplace was crackling inside. I tucked my face behind my paws.

I thought about what Callie had told me. The dog was outside, but here I was, outside, too! I could hear the puppy yapping in the backyard. If he kept that up, *he* would get to go back into the house. I would be the one stuck out here on the porch all night.

It was nearly dark when Mama finally let me in. I rubbed her leg. Putting my face near her knee, I pressed my whiskers against her. She picked me up and laid me on my back. I relaxed in her arms. Mama rubbed my tummy, chin, and face. It felt wonderful.

When she finally set me down, I ran for the food bowl. It was empty! Callie had eaten every bite! I meowed as loud as I could, then I trotted to the living room to tell Mama.

"Poor Gray! What's wrong with you?"

Mama followed me back to the kitchen. She found some scraps of meat and warm milk to put into the bowl. I gobbled it down, then headed for the bedroom. Callie had some explaining to do!

I hopped on the bed. All I could see was Callie's back.

"Hey, why didn't you leave me any cat food? I've been out in the cold most of the day. You always leave me plenty of food!"

"Bad Cats don't deserve good cat food!" Callie didn't even lift her head.

"I'm not a Bad Cat! You're the Bad Cat!" I whined.

Callie stretched slightly and looked me in the eye. "Do you know where the poor little puppy is?"

"Out in the cold, I hope!" I meowed.

"Guess again, Bad Cat! They put him out in the barn! He's so little. . . . The barn is so big

and empty." She turned her head to look at me. Her eyes narrowed. "It's all your fault, Bad Cat!"

A sudden chill raced from the base of my tail clear up to my ears. It was warm and cozy in the bedroom. The chill shot up my back again.

"Did you say 'the barn'?"

"The barn!" Callie repeated with a twitch of her nose.

My eyes flashed. I leaped from the bed and raced to the front door.

"Mee . . . ow!" I yowled. "Let me out. Let me out now!"

I ran to the playroom door. Mama was curled up on the couch with papers in her hands.

"Mee . . . owwww!" I howled.

"What is wrong with you, Cat?" Mama stood up and walked toward me.

"Let me out!" I led her to the front door.

Instead of opening the door, Mama picked me up and headed back toward the playroom.

"Mee . . . owwww! Let me out!" I struggled to get away from her. Twisting and turning, I managed to drop to the rug. I raced back to the door.

Daddy laid down the magazine he was reading. "He must be too hot with the fireplace going. Let him out. He'll want back in pretty quick!"

Callie appeared in the hall, trying to see what the commotion was.

I clawed at the wood on the front door. As soon as Mama opened it, I shot out. The icy air hit me in the face, but I scooted toward the lilac bushes.

Tiny whimpering sounds came from the barn.

It was *my* fault! I had to do something! I just hoped I wasn't too late.

CHAPTER 9

Ice covered the long branches of the lilac bushes that lined the driveway. The wind made it crackle as I raced by. I stopped at the barn, listening. There was no sound except for the puppy, whimpering inside. I gently crept toward the doorway. It was shut tight.

I raced around to the side of the barn. There was a hole, big enough for me to get in. I squeezed through and peered inside. Dark shadows were all that I could see. My ears perked, twitching and listening.

Soft whimpers came from the hay room. Watching for the rats, I wiggled my way through the opening and out of the wind.

Cautiously I wove between the piles of hay bales. Ratty scratching sounds came to my ears.

I called softly, "Meow! Where are you?"

Only limbs scraping against the walls of the barn answered me back.

"Puppy, where are you?" I called a little louder.

"Gray, is that you? Help me!"

I followed the soft sounds toward the back wall of the barn. I hopped up on top of two hay bales that were stacked there. I looked over. The pen was made out of hay. The barn served as one wall of the thing. Hay bales, one stacked on top of another, made the other three walls. Big brown eyes looked up at me. The puppy was shivering in a fuzzy, white heap near the back of the small pen.

"I'm so scared. Get me out of here!" He scooted even closer to the wall of hay. His whole body shook.

My slit eyes blinked, adjusting to the light in the barn. Nervous, I looked around. There were no signs of the rats.

The puppy whimpered again. "They've been watching me. They run past and show their ugly yellow teeth. Can you see them?"

Squinting, I looked into the cracks between the hay bales around the room. Small beady eyes gazed back. When I saw how tiny and frightened the eyes were, I almost purred.

"Mice . . . it's just mice!"

The puppy's tail gave one little wag. Then he

huddled down, trembling. He looked so small and helpless as he pressed himself between the hay and the huge wall of the barn.

"Gray, come closer to me. I am so scared. I want out of here."

I flipped my tail. "I'm watching for the rats. I don't have time for puppy games. You would wiggle and squirm all over the place."

"No, I won't! Please come down and help me get over the shivers." The puppy shook hard as he looked at me. "I'm so scared!"

"No puppy games! I've got to figure out what we are going to do."

"I promise! Just come closer and snuggle." The puppy's tail gave another wiggle, then stopped. He trembled all over.

I sprang quietly to the floor of the pen. Fluffing up my fur, I moved close to the pile of white. The small body nestled near me. Shivers came from him. After a time my body relaxed as the little pup fell asleep.

Helping him made me feel better, too. Maybe there was really nothing to worry about. Maybe the rats only came in the daytime and only ate the grain. Maybe the worried and scared I sensed was all for nothing.

My eyes felt heavy. I finally let them close and nestled closer to the white ball of fluff.

Suddenly my eyes sprang open. They darted

about the room, looking this way and that. Seeing nothing but the dim shadows, I blinked. I tried to close them, but they wouldn't shut.

There was a feeling—a presence—something . . . somewhere that made every muscle inside me spring tight. One of the dim shadows moved. It was high up on the wall of our pen. It crept on short, sneaky legs across one of the rafters at the very top of the barn. Another shadow trailed behind it. A long, ratty tail followed.

The dark forms disappeared. I held my breath. A soft crunching came from the hay. My throat made a gulping sound when I swallowed. Suddenly the ugly faces of two huge rats glared down at me from the top of the bales.

"Hey, look, we've been out in the cold night, and dinner has been right here waiting for us." The largest rat flicked his long tail.

"Yeah, nice fat little puppies. Double treat! Yummy!"

"I'm starving, let's eat! Two free dinners!"

I watched as the big rats moved closer. The larger one stopped. Frowning, he leaned over the edge of the hay bale.

"Hey, Smitty, one of these little treats is a cat. A pretty big cat! I think we can take them, but maybe we'd better get the rest of the gang before we start!"

"I think we can take him. He's been in here before, and he always runs away. I don't think he'll give us any trouble."

I scrunched up all the courage that I could. I was a cat. I was brave. I sprang to my feet. Only when I did, my legs shook so hard I thought I was going to fall over.

"Come on down here, you big cowards!" I hissed and snarled. "I'm bigger than you think! I can take you both on!"

The smaller rat twitched her whiskers. "He's not running, Smitty."

"He will," the other rat whispered back. "He's scared."

I forced my legs to stay still. I wouldn't run! My legs shook harder. Okay, I wouldn't run, but if my legs kept shaking—I might fall over.

The big rat looked over his shoulder. "Maybe we should get Joe and Charlene—just in case."

Two ratty faces gazed down long pointed noses at us. "Stay put, little treats! We'll be right back for supper!"

They turned and scurried away. Above us I could see the shadows creeping across the rafters of the barn. The shadows were huge! The rats were huge!

"Gray, what are we going to do? They are going to get some more rats to eat us up!" The puppy

started shaking all over again. "I don't want to be rat food!"

"We're not going to be rat food, pup! I'll think of something, just give me a minute to figure this out!" I tried to sound brave, but inside I was shaking as much as the puppy.

It wasn't long before I heard the scratchy sounds of rat feet coming back toward us. Suddenly I knew what I had to do!

With a big leap I jumped from the small pen, scampered across the barn, and shot through the hole near the grain bin.

I ran!

CHAPTER 10

Icy wind hit my face as I ran past the lilac bushes. Dark shadows covered the front yard. I sprang to the window ledge.

"Meow! Help! Come help me!" I yowled as loud as I could. The red embers in the fireplace burned low. No one was in the front room.

I jumped to the porch. With my claws I scratched at the front door. Someone always came when I tore at the wood. I backed up and waited.

"Meee . . . ow! Help me!"

I dashed through the holly bushes. Squeezing between the house and the fence, I felt the wires scratch at my skin. It hurt, really bad, but I didn't stop. I looked for the window where Callie slept. Jumping on the ledge, I yowled for her.

"Mee . . . ow! Callie! The puppy needs help! Hurry!"

I rushed back to the fence. My side really hurt from where the wire had grabbed me, so I decided to jump over this time.

When I got to the front door, I waited for them to let me in. I swished my tail and tried to be patient. The light should come on first.

No one came to the door. I had to get help!

I jumped over the fence again and into the backyard. Once more on the ledge, I began to scratch as hard as I could against the wire mesh.

"Meee . . . *Ow!*" I howled.

Callie's nose pushed through the window blinds. "What's wrong with you, you crazy cat? Do you want to wake up Mama and Daddy?"

"Hurry! I need you to help me. The rats are after the puppy!"

"I don't think I can fight rats anymore, but I'll try my best!"

Callie's nose disappeared. Suddenly the blinds shot up into the air.

"Get down, Gray! You're tearing up the screen!" Daddy tried to shoo me away.

"*Meee . . . oooow!* The puppy needs help! Meee . . . ow!"

Daddy opened the window. "Scat, you crazy thing. You should have stayed in when you had the chance!"

"I'll let him in. It must be freezing out there for him to carry on that way!"

I could see Mama putting on her big fluffy robe. I hurried back over the fence and ran to the door. When it opened, I spun around and dashed back toward the barn.

"Meee . . . *ow!* Help the puppy!"

"Gray! Come here, kitty!" Mama yelled at me.

I came back toward her, then darted for the barn again.

"Something is wrong, Owen! Isn't that blood on the porch?"

Callie shot out the door. "Come on, Gray, let's go!"

"The door is shut. We have to go in through the crack by the grain bin. Hurry."

"You go ahead, Gray. I can't keep up. My legs aren't as strong as they used to be. Go on!"

The place where the fence wire cut my side made me flinch when I squeezed through the crack in the barn. I stopped. Held my breath. Listened. There was nothing but silence inside the barn.

Maybe I'm too late. Maybe I should have stayed, instead of going for help. Maybe the rats had already . . .

I couldn't think about it. It was too horrible to imagine. I raced across the hay-covered floor, leaped over the bales of the puppy's pen, and braced myself for the terrible sight.

"I thought you had left me forever, Gray!" The puppy wagged his fuzzy tail.

I sighed, relieved to see him still okay. Fact was, I was so happy to see him, I gave him a little kiss on the cheek with my tongue. (Puppies don't taste too good.)

"The rats didn't come back?"

The puppy shook his head.

Perking my ears, I listened. Scratching sounds came. Shadows crept across the wall and the ceiling. Then the shadows were gone. I could hear them. They were close, but I couldn't see them. I leaned against the puppy. With my back end I pushed him into the corner by the wall. The attack would come from the hay bales. I kept myself between the hay and him.

The little furball leaned against me! I could hear ratty feet getting nearer.

Sharp little noses pushed their way over the hay bale. The ugly faces of Nora and Smitty peered at us. Beady eyes stared from behind them. In all, seven big rats were ready to pounce!

I knew we were goners! Callie and my people weren't coming. The puppy and I were all alone. Suddenly my trembling stopped. I took a deep breath. *They might get me,* I thought. *But they weren't going to get the puppy. Not without a fight.*

I puffed up my fur as big as I could! "Phsssst!" I hissed at them.

"Look at the *big* kitty!" Nora mocked. "He thinks he can scare us! He doesn't know how smart we are! We have our Ph.D.s!"

"Yeah," Smitty agreed. "We've all been well trained in People Habitat Destruction. Anything people have or depend on, we can destroy."

"We sneak into their homes and eat their food," one rat said.

"We steal the grain that their cows and chickens eat," another chimed in.

"We even know how to chew the wiring that brings light to their homes." A third one chuckled. "Anything people have, we can destroy."

Nora crept closer. "One of the things we learn from our Ph.D. program is to get rid of cats and dogs—while they're little. If we wait until they're big, it makes it harder for us to tear up things." She turned to smile at the others. "Let's get the dumb cat first!"

Smitty's bald head shined as he crept up beside her.

The other rats began to circle around us on the hay bales. I could see the light glint in their cold black eyes.

"Phsssssst! Get back! We can take care of ourselves!"

The fuzzy puppy snapped with his little teeth, making a funny chomping sound.

The big rats moved closer. One step at a time—closer and closer and . . .

"MMEEEOOW!"

Suddenly light filled the barn. It was so bright, my eyes blinked. When I opened them again, I saw Callie. She jumped up behind the biggest rat! She slapped Smitty's rear with her sharp claws.

The other rats began to move back as Smitty yelled in pain.

"Oh, my gosh! Look at all the rats!" Mama screamed.

Daddy grabbed the pitchfork near the side door.

Mama scooped up the puppy and me in her fluffy blue robe and hurried toward the house.

I struggled to get free. Callie needed my help. She was old. There were seven rats. Mama wouldn't loosen her grip. I finally struggled high enough on her shoulder so I could see over.

Callie had Smitty in her sharp teeth. Daddy was whacking at something with a big stick. Except for Nora the others had disappeared into the darkness. I could see her glaring back at me from the barn rafters. A little smile covered her face when our eyes met. Despite the chill her look left inside me, I glared back.

Mama stood just inside the doorway of the house. She held us so tight we were kind of smushed together. The puppy licked my face.

"Hey, you promised. None of that puppy stuff!"

"Thank you for saving me!" he yipped. "I was so scared, and I thought that you had left me for those big rats. They were going to eat me in one bite. Thank you, Gray!" His pink tongue licked at me again.

Mama was still standing inside the door holding us when Daddy and Callie came in.

"There were too many of them. Callie got one and I got one, but the rest got away. I think that crazy cat was trying to save the puppy!"

"I didn't think Gray liked the puppy. But look at them now!" Mama was holding us a little close. The dumb puppy kept licking me so much that my fur was getting wet.

Mama carried us into the kitchen and settled us into the box of towels. The puppy nuzzled up to me. I curled around him to keep him warm.

Maybe he wasn't so bad after all. He had tried to keep the rats back. Maybe when we got bigger we could go hunting together.

Being friends with a dog might not be so bad after all.

ABOUT THE AUTHORS

High school sweethearts, **Carol Wallace** and **Bill Wallace** have raised three children: Laurie, Nikki, and Justin. They live on the family farm near Chickasha, Oklahoma, with six dogs, one cat, one horse, and one albino rat snake.

Carol taught second grade for twenty-six years. When she left the teaching profession, she planned to spend her time relaxing and cleaning closets. That got old—real quick. The family cat, Gray, was a constant source of entertainment. Carol had lots of anecdotes about the pet. Not sure how to share those stories, Carol had Bill help her write the first book about Gray, *The Flying Flea, Callie, and Me.*

At home, Bill and Carol try to keep up with their animals, their writing, and their granddaughters, Kristine and Bethany. Part of their time is spent traveling to speak at schools and conferences throughout the United States.

Chomps, their Scottish terrier, joins in the fun for this—their second book about their loving cat, Gray.

Don't Miss These Fun Animal Adventures from

BILL WALLACE

UPCHUCK AND THE ROTTEN WILLY

Cats and dogs just can't be friends—or can they?

Iowa Children's Choice Award Master List 2000-2001
Indian Paintbrush Award Master List 1999-2000
Nevada Young Readers Award Master List 1999-2000

UPCHUCK AND THE ROTTEN WILLY: THE GREAT ESCAPE

It's a dog's life—as told by a cat.

UPCHUCK AND THE ROTTEN WILLY: RUNNING WILD

It's not so bad living a dog's life. Unless you're a cat.

 A MINSTREL® BOOK

Available from Minstrel® Books
Published by Pocket Books

2300-02